SPACE EXPLORERS

THE STARS

Giles Sparrow

Published in 2018 by Enslow Publishing, LLC.
101 W. 23rd Street, Suite 240, New York, NY 10011

Library of Congress Cataloging-in-Publication Data

Names: Sparrow, Giles, 1970- author.
Title: The stars / Giles Sparrow.
Description: New York, NY : Enslow Publishing, 2018. | Series: Space explorers | Audience: K to grade 3. | Includes bibliographical references and index.
Identifiers: LCCN 2017031494| ISBN 9780766092655 (library bound) | ISBN 9780766094048 (pbk.) | ISBN 9780766094055 (6 pack)
Subjects: LCSH: Stars—Juvenile literature.
Classification: LCC QB801.7 .S628 2018 | DDC 523.8—dc23
LC record available at https://lccn.loc.gov/2017031494

Printed in the United States of America

To Our Readers: We have done our best to make sure all websites in this book were active and appropriate when we went to press. However, the author and the publisher have no control over and assume no liability for the material available on those websites or on any websites they may link to. Any comments or suggestions can be sent by e-mail to customerservice@enslow.com.

Picture Credits:
Key: b-bottom, t-top, c-center, l-left, r-right alexfreire: 16br & 27tl; ESA: 6cr (D Ducros); ESO: 12c (L Calçada), 21b (Y Beletsky); Keck Observatory: 25cr (NRC-HIA, Christian Marois); NASA: 8-9 (Digitized Sky Survey, Noel Carboni), 14b & cover/title page br & 31bl, 15tr & 26br (HST/ASU/J Hester et al.), 16c (AEI/ZIB/M Koppitz & L Rezzolla), 18br & 27tr (HST), 22c & 27br (ESA/S Larsen), 24b & 27bl (ESA/ESO/L Ricci), 25tc & 31br (CXC/M Weiss), 29 tr; Shutterstock: cover & title page main (Triff), tl (Antares_StarExplorer), tr (mikolajn), cr (Tragoolchitr Jittasaiyapan), 4-5 (Stefano Garau), 4cl & 31tr (MaraQu), 4b (Viktar Malyshchyts), 4cr (NASA), 5t (tose), 5br (pixbox77), 6-7 (My Good Images), 9br (sciencepics), 10-11 (ESA/NASA/Herschel/Hubble/DSS), 11tl & 26bl (ESO/VPHAS+ Consortium/ Cambridge Astronomical Survey Unit), 11tc (Egyptian Studio/NASA), 11tr & 26cr (Ken Crawford Rancho Del Sol Observatory), 12-13 (Kalabi Yau), 12br (Jurik Peter), 13tr (sciencepics), 14-15 & cover/title page cl (Jurik Peter), 16-17 (Vadim Sadovski), 17br (Catmando), 18-19 (Ken Crawford), 20-21 (Valerio Pardi), 22-23 (Tragoolchitr Jittasaiyapan), 24-25 (Giovanni Benintende), 26tl (solarseven), 28b (Denis Belitsky), 29cl (Bill Frische), 29 br (snapgalleria); Wikimedia Commons: 7br & 27tr (NASA/ESA/ G Bacon/STScl), 20c & 27cl (Henryk Kowalewski).

Enslow Publishing
101 W. 23rd Street
Suite 240
New York, NY 10011
USA
enslow.com

CONTENTS

Introduction

Our Universe is a huge area of space made up of everything we can see in every direction. It contains a great number of different objects—from tiny specks of cosmic dust to mighty galaxy superclusters. The most interesting of these are planets, stars and nebulae, galaxies, and clusters of galaxies.

Stars

A star is a dense (tightly packed) ball of gas that shines through chemical reactions in its core (middle). Our Sun is a star. Stars range from red dwarfs, much smaller and fainter than the Sun, to supergiants a hundred times larger and a million times brighter.

Planets

A planet is a large ball of rock or gas that orbits (travels around) a star. In our solar system there are eight "major" planets, several dwarf planets, and countless smaller objects. These range from asteroids and comets down to tiny specks of dust.

Nebulae

The space between the stars is filled with mostly unseen clouds of gas and dust called nebulae. Where they collapse (fall in) and grow dense enough to form new stars, they light up from within.

Galaxies

A galaxy is a huge cloud of stars, gas, and dust, including nebulae, held together by a force called gravity. There are many different types of galaxy. This is because their shape, the nature of their stars, and the amount of gas and dust within them can vary.

This is our home galaxy, the Milky Way, seen from Earth. Our view of the Universe depends on what we can see using the best technologies that we have.

Galaxy Clusters

Gravity makes galaxies bunch together to form clusters that are millions of light-years wide. These clusters join together at the edges to form even bigger superclusters—the largest structures in the Universe.

Stars

Almost every light you see in the night sky is a star (apart from satellites or aircrafts). Stars are the only objects in the Universe that truly shine, or make their own light. Everything else, from planets to glowing clouds of gas, is only reflecting or absorbing (taking in) starlight.

Star Power

A star is simply a huge ball of gas that shines by changing light chemical elements (usually hydrogen) into heavier ones (usually helium). The process is called nuclear fusion, but astronomers still talk about stars "burning" their fuel supplies.

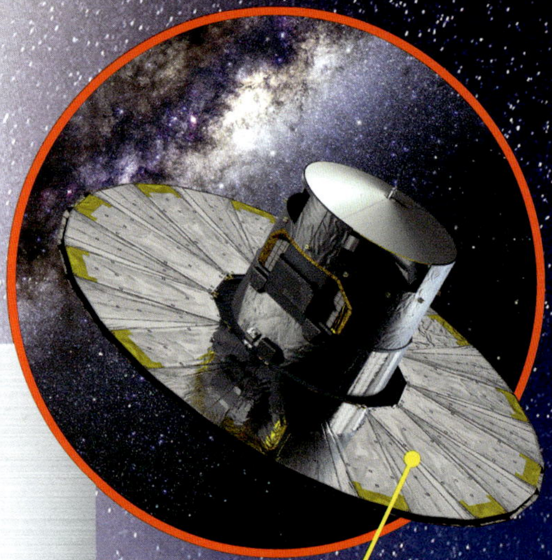

The *Gaia* satellite uses tiny changes in the position of stars to work out how far away they are.

Measuring Stars

Even powerful telescopes cannot turn most stars into anything more than pinpricks of light, but astronomers can still find out an amazing amount. The wavelengths of light that a star releases can tell us about its surface temperature and chemical make-up. The star's movement in the sky compared to other stars can show its mass, and perhaps its distance from Earth.

TELESCOPE PROFILE

Name: *Gaia*
Launched: 2013
Mirror diameter: 4.8 x 1.6 ft (1.45 x 0.5 m)
Weight: 3,069 lb (1,392 kg)
Mission duration: Five years (planned)
Description: *Gaia* will measure the exact positions of one billion stars in the Milky Way.

The stars visible with the naked eye can be just a few light-years away or more than a thousand.

A star's brightness in the sky is called its magnitude. The brighter a star, the lower its magnitude.

Stars vary in brightness. Dwarfs are a thousand times fainter than the Sun, and giants are a million times brighter.

Sirius, the Dog Star, is the brightest star in the sky and one of the closest (8.6 light-years away). It has a faint twin star called Sirius B.

Types of Stars

The fact that stars have very different brightnesses and vary in hue from red to blue tells us that they are very different from each other. A star's brightness depends on the amount of energy it produces. Its tint tells us the temperature of its surface—red stars are cool, yellow stars hotter, and blue stars the hottest of all.

The Main Sequence

When you look at a large enough number of stars, a pattern starts to show. Cool red stars are fainter and hot blue ones are much brighter. Bright red stars are very rare, and so are faint blue ones. The link between temperature and energy output lasts for most of a star's lifetime. Astronomers call it the "main sequence" relationship.

The Witch Head Nebula is a cloud of dust and gas close to Rigel that shines by reflecting the star's light.

STAR PROFILE

Name: Rigel
Distance: 860 light-years
Constellation: Orion
Mass: 23 Suns
Brightness: At least 120,000 Suns
Surface temperature: 21,800 °F (12,100 °C)
Star type: Blue supergiant

Life Spans of Stars

Exactly where a star sits on the "main sequence" depends on its mass, just how much fuel it has, and how fast it burns. Low-mass stars called red dwarfs burn their fuel very slowly and so can shine for tens of billions of years. Middling ones like our Sun use up their fuel in about ten billion years. Really massive stars burn fast and bright, lasting just a few million years.

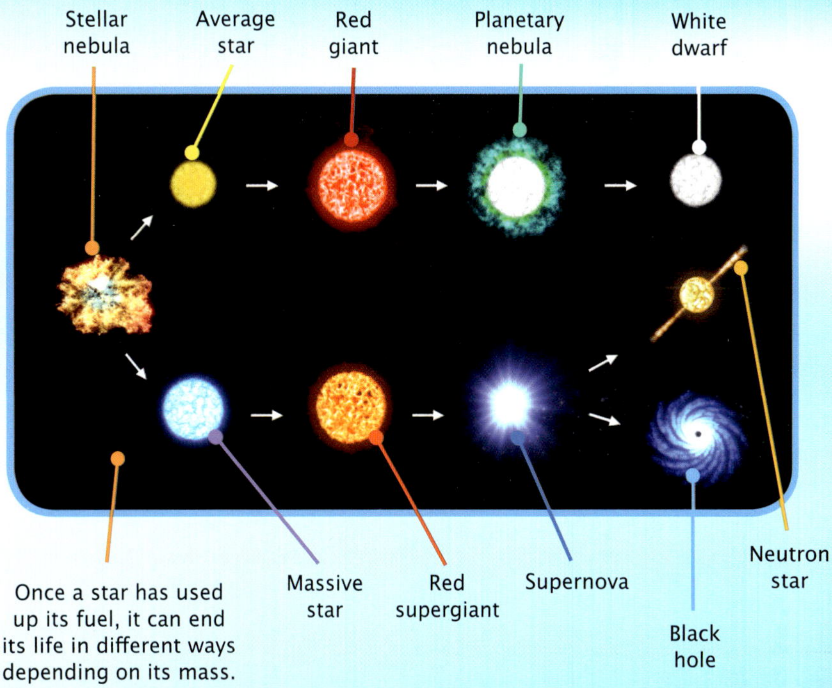

Once a star has used up its fuel, it can end its life in different ways depending on its mass.

Star Birth

Stars are born in huge clouds of gas and dust called nebulae. They begin their lives as collapsing knots of gas that grow hotter and denser for perhaps a million years, until conditions at the core are able to turn hydrogen into helium.

Brought into Being

Star-birth nebulae are some of the most beautiful sights in the Universe. As the stars inside begin to shine, they make the gas nearby glow. Different elements create red, green, yellow, and other hues. Streams of particles blowing off the surface of the stars shape their surroundings into all kinds of shapes.

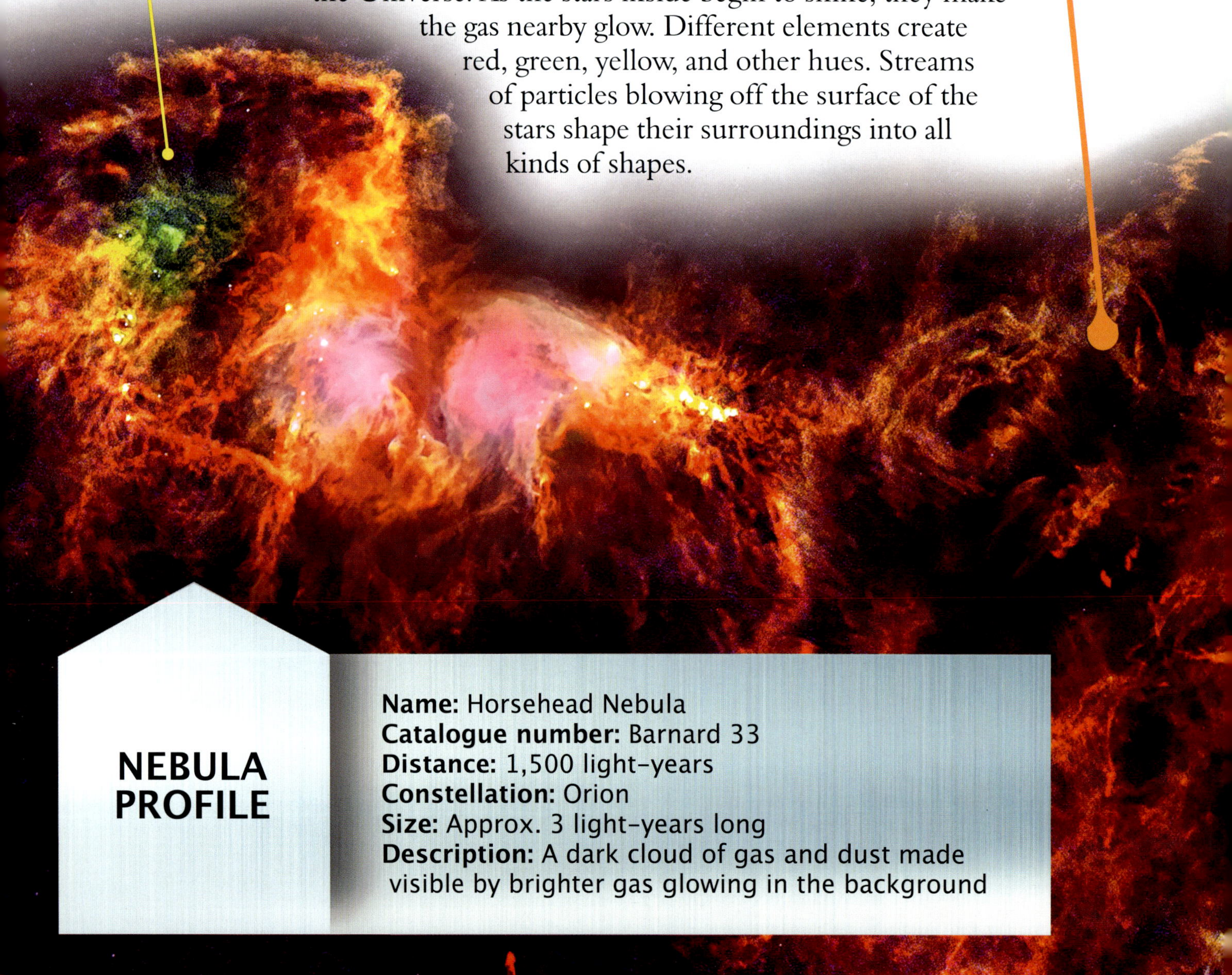

An infrared view of part of the Horsehead Nebula region of Orion.

Infrared shines through the dust to show glowing gas, warmed by newborn stars.

NEBULA PROFILE

Name: Horsehead Nebula
Catalogue number: Barnard 33
Distance: 1,500 light-years
Constellation: Orion
Size: Approx. 3 light-years long
Description: A dark cloud of gas and dust made visible by brighter gas glowing in the background

STAR-FORMING NEBULAE

Carina

This nebula is the largest and brightest in the sky, but is visible only in southern skies.

Eagle

Stars are born inside these towers of gas and dust in the constellation Serpens, the Snake.

Horsehead

Seen as a whole, the famous Horsehead Nebula in Orion looks like a chesspiece.

The Horsehead is just one part of a much larger star factory.

Star Death

When a star runs out of hydrogen to burn in its core, it is the beginning of the end. Stars have different ways to keep shining for a while longer, but they all run out of energy in the end. What happens next depends on the mass of the star.

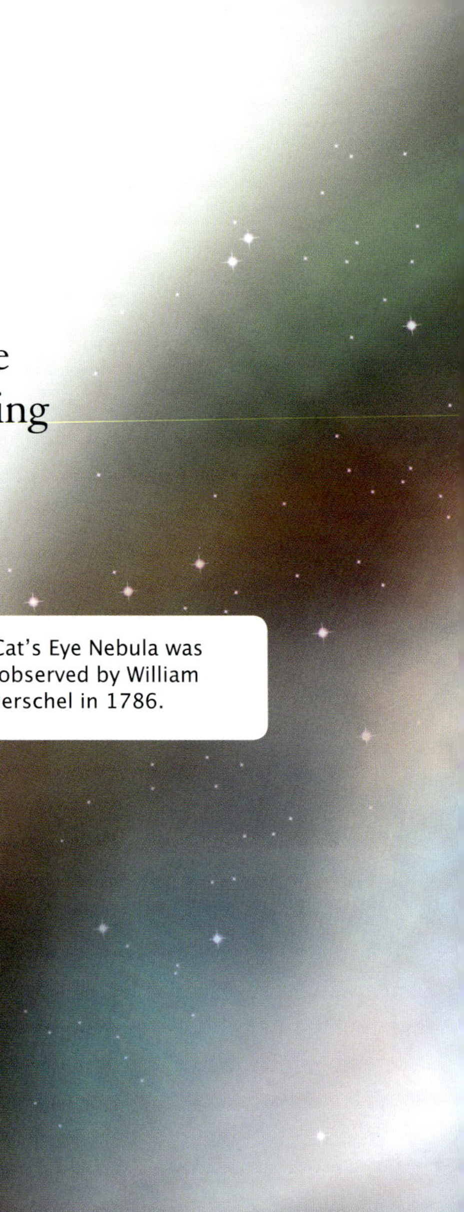

The Cat's Eye Nebula was first observed by William Herschel in 1786.

Red Giants

As its main fuel supply runs out, a star goes through many internal (inside) changes. Its core actually gets hotter and it starts to burn hydrogen closer to the surface. This makes the star brighter, but it also makes it grow very large, so its surface is farther away from the hot core and cools. It is now a red giant.

Betelgeuse in the constellation Orion is a red supergiant star.

Explosive Death

A star with about the mass of our own Sun never makes it past the red giant stage. As it grows, it starts to vibrate (quickly grow bigger and then smaller again and again). In the end, it throws off its outer layers. High-mass stars, however, keep burning fuel and making heavier elements in their cores. When they become unstable, this leads to a sudden and violent explosion called a supernova.

Supernova explosions are rare, but can outshine an entire galaxy for a short while.

Over millions of years, white dwarfs slowly lose their heat and turn into black dwarfs.

The Cat's Eye is a beautiful planetary nebula created as a dying, Sun-like star blows out complex bubbles of gas during its last years.

NEBULA PROFILE

Name: Cat's Eye Nebula
Catalogue number: NGC 6543
Distance: 3,300 light-years
Constellation: Draco
Size: Approx 0.5 light-years wide
Description: A planetary nebula with complex bubbles that may be shaped by an unseen twin star

Neutron Stars

Neutron stars are all that is left behind when a supernova tears a monster star apart at the end of its life. They have the mass of a star like our own Sun, tightly packed into a sphere (ball) the size of a city.

Cosmic Lighthouses

As a star's core breaks into a neutron star, its rotation speeds up a lot. At the same time, its magnetic field grows much stronger, until it forces all of the star's radiation into two thin beams. The neutron star has become a flashing cosmic lighthouse called a pulsar.

The fastest pulsars spin hundreds of times per second.

Inside a Neutron Star

During a supernova explosion, a giant star's core is compressed (squeezed) with so much force that its atoms break down completely. Subatomic particles (smaller than an atom) called protons and electrons, with positive and negative electric charges, are then forced together to make uncharged neutrons. The neutrons stop the star from breaking apart by knocking into each other.

The searing-hot surface of a neutron star gives off most of its energy as X-rays.

The Crab Pulsar is a neutron star at the heart of the famous Crab Nebula in the constellation of Taurus, the Bull.

A neutron star's magnetism forces its radiation into two beams—as it spins, these sweep across the sky like lighthouse beams. This flashing star is called a pulsar.

The pulsar is surrounded by debris that flew off during the supernova explosion.

STAR PROFILE

Name: Crab Pulsar
Distance: 7,200 light-years
Constellation: Taurus
Mass: 1.4 Suns
Rotation period: 29.8 times per second (33.5 ms)
Temperature: 2.9 million °F (1.6 million °C)
Star type: Neutron star

Black Holes

The strangest objects in the Universe, black holes are formed by the death of the largest stars of all. With gravity so strong that not even light can escape, they pull anything that passes too close to its doom. A blast of radiation is the only sign the object was ever there.

Birth of a Black Hole

When the core of a dying giant star breaks apart (collapses) and has more than twice the mass of the Sun, it does not stop collapsing at the neutron star stage. Instead, the neutrons themselves are torn apart and the core shrinks to a tiny size. As its gravity grows strong enough to prevent light from escaping, it forms a black hole.

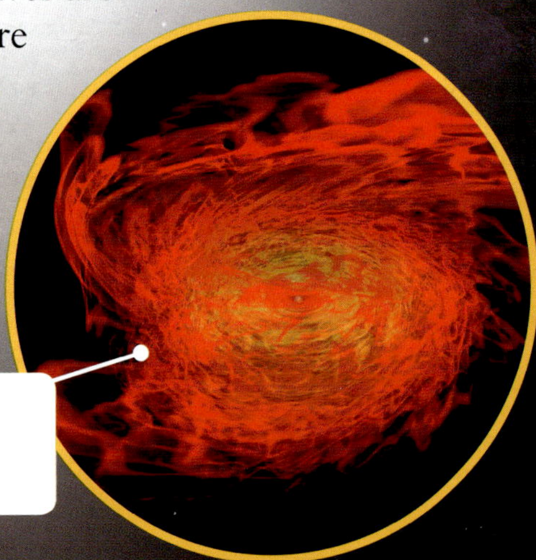

A computer image shows two black holes joining together.

A black hole itself is almost invisible. However, as it feeds it creates a disk of superhot material that releases X-rays as it spirals inward.

SPACECRAFT PROFILE

Name: *Chandra X-ray Observatory*
Launched: 1999
Mirror diameter: 3.9 ft (1.2 m)
Weight: 10,560 lb (4,790 kg)
Description: NASA's main X-ray observatory, which has discovered many new black holes

Twisted magnetic fields around black holes can create jets of particles that shoot out into space.

The Event Horizon

The black hole has a border, called its event horizon, that seals the core off from the rest of the Universe. Once it reaches the event horizon, an object has to travel faster than light to escape the black hole's pull. Inside the black hole, the core may carry on collapsing to a point in space called a singularity.

Interstellar Space

The space between the stars is far from empty—it's full of gas, dust, and particles that form the raw material for new stars. In this way, our galaxy and others are like massive recyclers, remixing the same material and repackaging it into new stars.

Cosmic Recycling

Since the birth of the Universe, each new star has added more heavy elements to the light ones that formed in the Big Bang. These include elements such as oxygen and carbon, which make up our planet and play a key role in life itself. We are all made of star stuff.

The Western Veil Nebula is a growing bubble of debris released by a supernova explosion more than 5,000 years ago.

Cycles of Star Birth

Astronomers think that star birth is often started when shockwaves from earlier supernova explosions meet clouds of star-forming material. Growing supernova debris also adds heavy elements to the star-forming nebula. Some elements end up in the new stars, and others form planets.

Heavy elements form the dark dust in star-forming particles.

NEBULA PROFILE

Name: Western Veil Nebula
Catalogue number: NGC 6960
Distance: 1,470 light-years
Constellation: Cygnus
Size: Approx 90 light-years wide
Description: The remains of a supernova that covers 36 times the area of a Full Moon

Gas in the expanding (growing) nebula is heated to temperatures of 270,000 °F (150,000 °C).

The remains of the supernova are made up of elements including hydrogen, oxygen, and carbon. These will one day find their way into new stars.

Star Groups

Stars are born together in "nurseries" of star-forming nebulae, so they are usually found in loose groups called open clusters. Over tens of millions of years, these star clouds slowly drift apart, but some stars stick together all their lives.

Binaries and Multiples

Sometimes, the slowly spinning clumps of gas that form stars split into two or more regions. Each of these can then give birth to a star, leading to a pair or group of stars locked in orbit around each other. This is called a binary or multiple system. Because their stars were born at the same time, these systems can tell us a lot about the life cycles of stars.

Starlight reflects off nearby dust to surround the Pleiades with a blue glow.

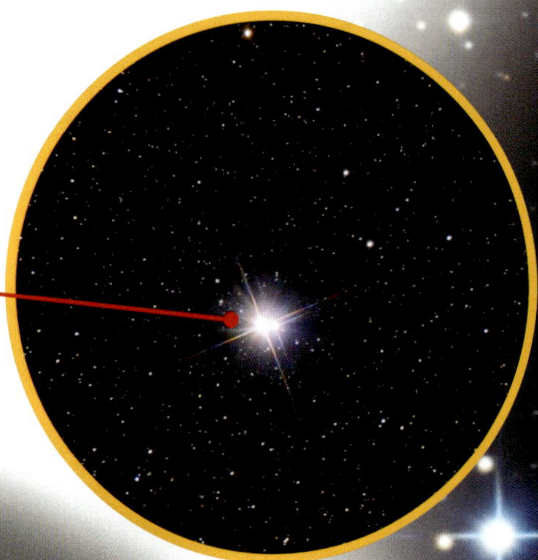

Albireo in the constellation Cygnus, the Swan, is a beautiful binary pair of blue and orange stars.

CLUSTER PROFILE

Name: Pleiades or Seven Sisters
Catalogue number: Messier 45
Distance: 450 light-years
Constellation: Taurus
Size: Approx 30 light-years wide
Description: A cluster of at least 1,000 stars that formed together about 100 million years ago

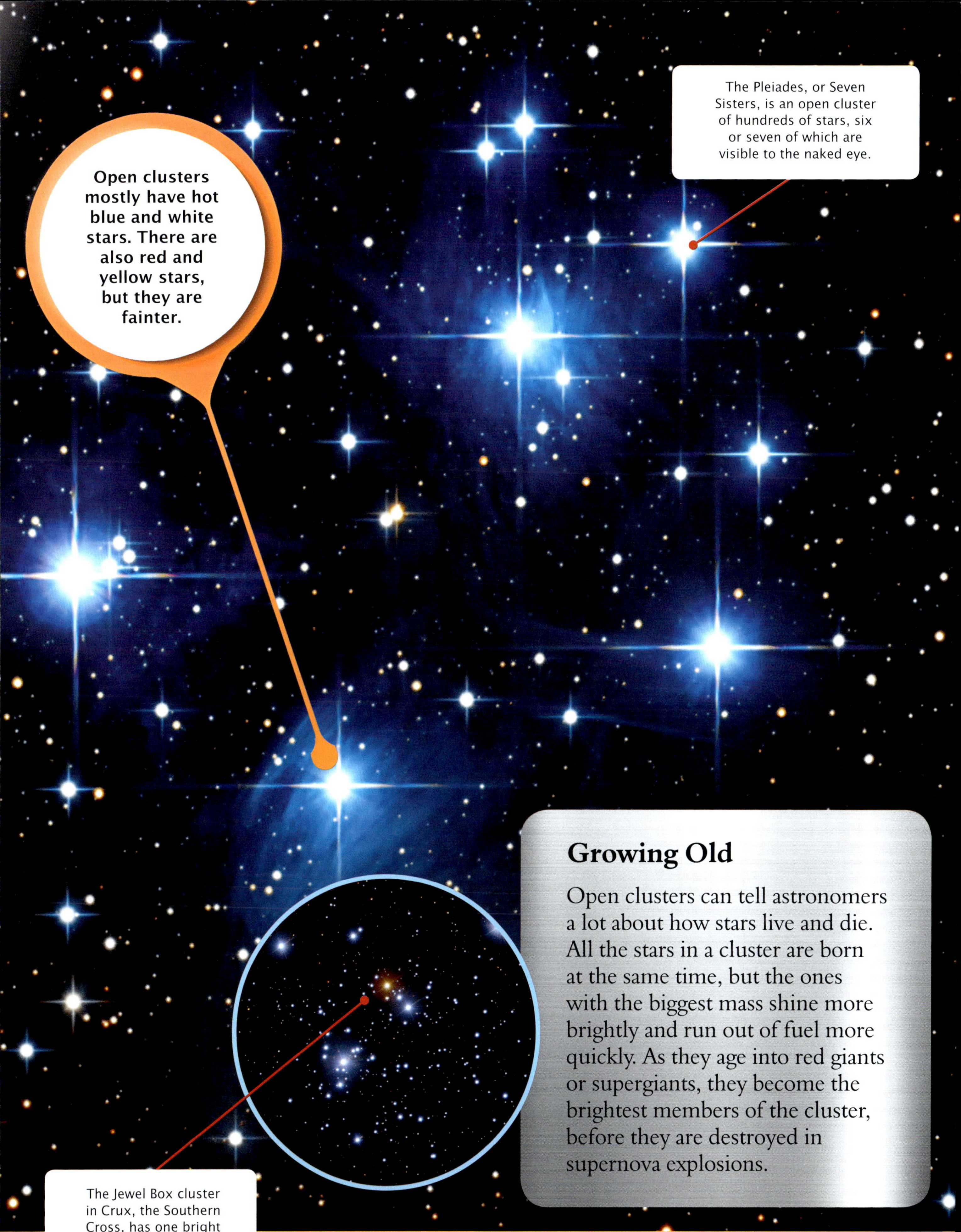

The Pleiades, or Seven Sisters, is an open cluster of hundreds of stars, six or seven of which are visible to the naked eye.

Open clusters mostly have hot blue and white stars. There are also red and yellow stars, but they are fainter.

The Jewel Box cluster in Crux, the Southern Cross, has one bright red member.

Growing Old

Open clusters can tell astronomers a lot about how stars live and die. All the stars in a cluster are born at the same time, but the ones with the biggest mass shine more brightly and run out of fuel more quickly. As they age into red giants or supergiants, they become the brightest members of the cluster, before they are destroyed in supernova explosions.

Globular Clusters

Very different from open star clusters, globular clusters are tight, compact balls with tens or hundreds of thousands of stars closely packed together. The stars in globular clusters are ancient compared to most of the ones we see in other parts of the galaxy.

Some astronomers think that Omega Centauri might be the core of a galaxy torn apart by the Milky Way.

Distant Blobs

Globular clusters are much more difficult to see in the sky than open clusters and are many thousands of light-years away from Earth. They are only found around the middle of our galaxy and above and below its disk in a region called the halo. Their small size (usually a few tens of light-years across), means they look like fuzzy blobs.

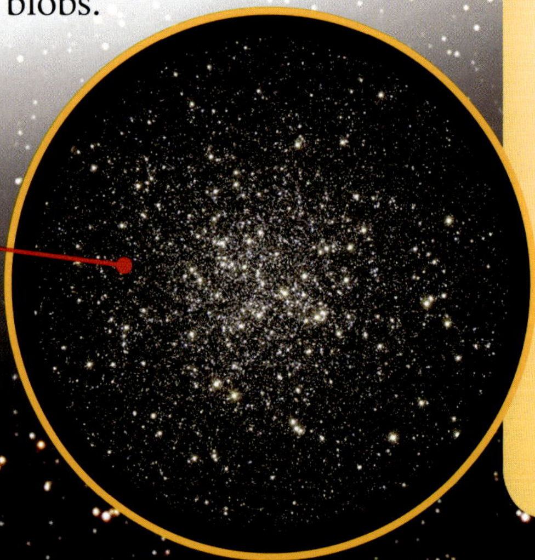

Messier 13 in the constellation of Hercules is the brightest globular cluster in the northern sky.

Globular Beginnings

The old stars in globular clusters are red and yellow, and less massive than the Sun. There are no young hot stars, and no star-forming gas. Astronomers think that globulars formed during ancient galaxy collisions that created huge star clusters. While heavier stars in these clusters aged and died, the longer-lived, red and yellow stars survived until today.

CLUSTER PROFILE

Name: Omega Centauri
Catalogue number: NGC 5139
Distance: 15,800 light-years
Constellation: Centaurus
Size: Approx 150 light-years wide
Description: The largest and densest of the Milky Way's globular clusters, with about ten million stars

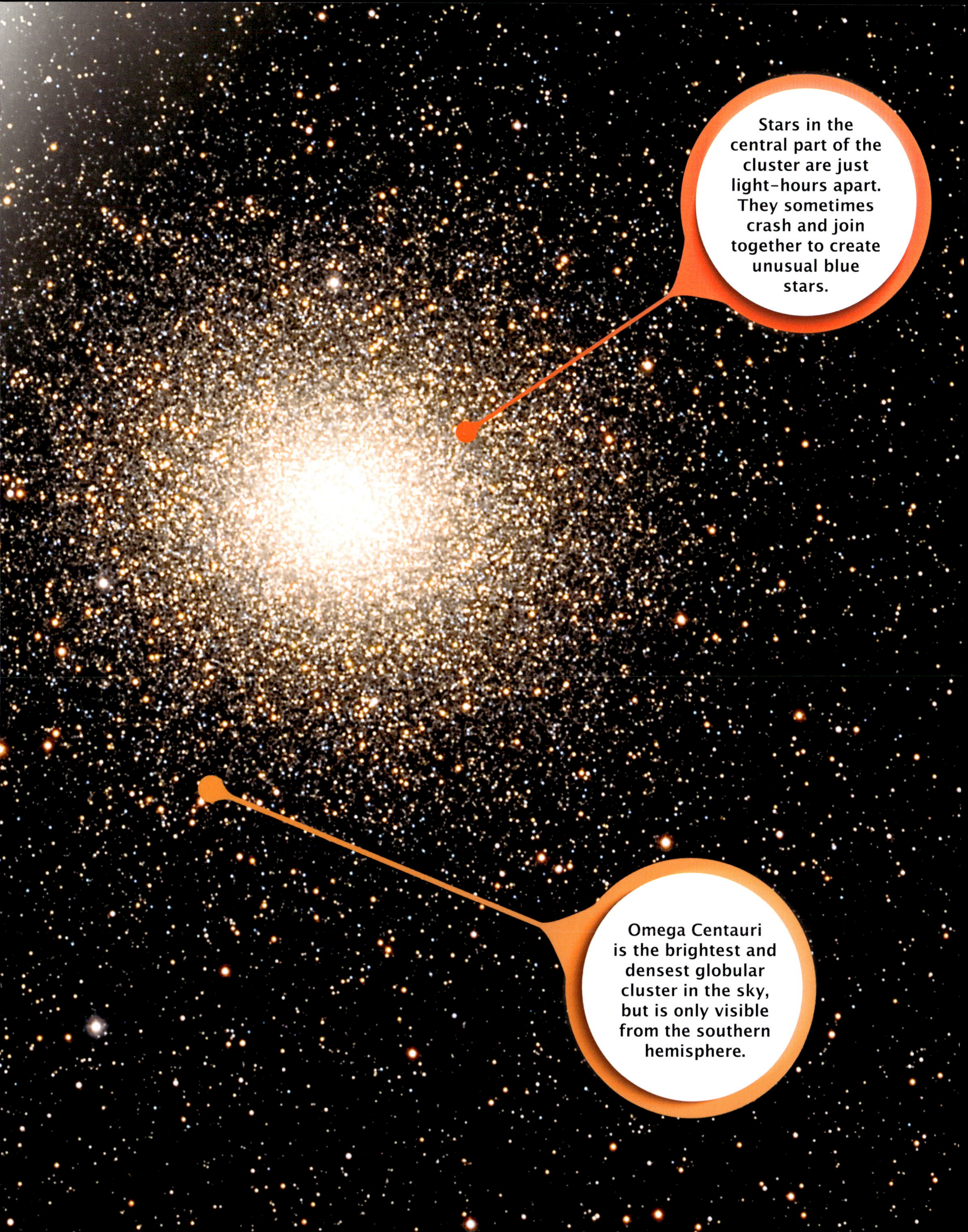

Stars in the central part of the cluster are just light-hours apart. They sometimes crash and join together to create unusual blue stars.

Omega Centauri is the brightest and densest globular cluster in the sky, but is only visible from the southern hemisphere.

Exoplanets

Over the past few years, astronomers have discovered more than a thousand exoplanets—planets orbiting stars outside our solar system. They have also found signs of many more being born, but these worlds are often very different from Earth.

Planets form in nebulae that are rich in dust made from heavier elements, such as that in the Orion Nebula.

How Planets are Born

As stars leave their birth nebulae, they are often surrounded by a flattened disk called a proplyd. Over time, the material in this disk starts to clump together until some clumps have enough gravity to pull in more gas and dust from their surroundings. Once this has happened, they quickly grow into protoplanets, which crash and form planets.

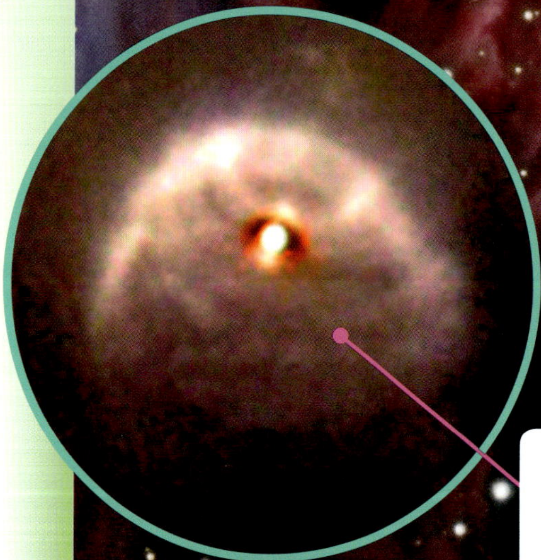

The *Hubble Space Telescope* discovered that many newborn stars in the Orion Nebula are surrounded by proplyds.

Planet Hunting

Astronomers use two main methods to look for planets. One way is to look for the tiny wobbles in a star's movement that are caused by an orbiting planet pulling it in different directions. Another is to watch for tiny dips in a star's brightness that happen when a planet is passing in front of it. With both methods it is easier to find giant planets, similar to Jupiter, rather than smaller ones.

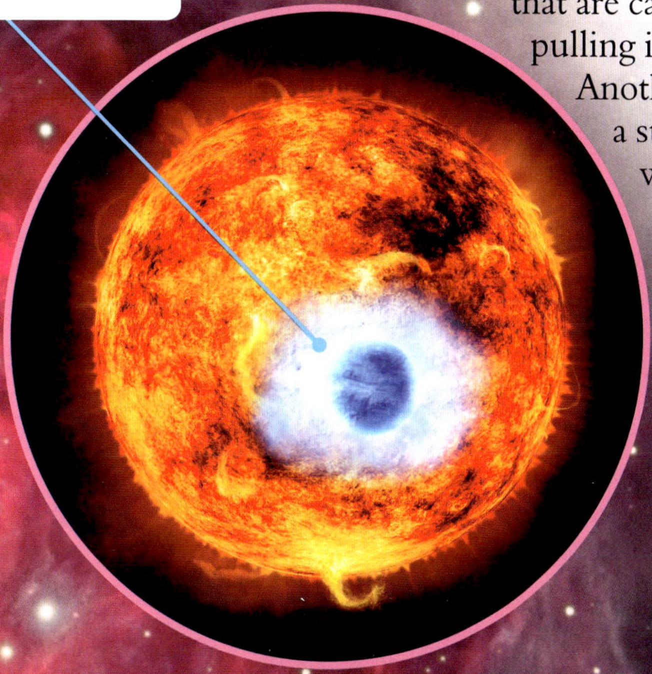

Planet hunters have found a lot of "hot Jupiters"—giant exoplanets orbiting very near their stars.

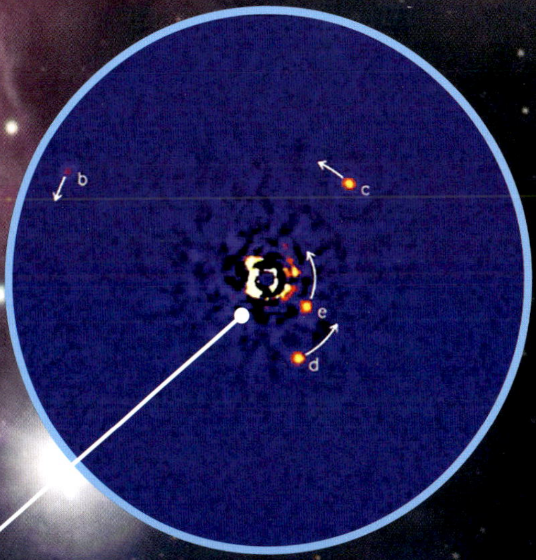

This image of a planetary system called HR8799 was taken by the Keck Telescope.

NEBULA PROFILE

Name: Orion Nebula
Catalogue number: Messier 42
Distance: 1,340 light-years
Constellation: Orion
Size: Approx 25 light-years wide
Description: The heart of a huge star-forming region that spreads across Orion

Did You Know?

There's always more to learn about what lies in the vastness of space. Boost your knowledge with these amazing facts about the stars.

Sirius B is the **white dwarf** left behind by a star that was once brighter than Sirius itself.

The Sun is about halfway through its ten billion years on the main sequence. After that it will swell to a **red giant** and may swallow the Earth!

Much of the constellation of Orion is filled with star-forming **gas clouds**, including the famous Orion Nebula.

Planetary nebulae are short-lived compared to other objects in space—while some stars shine for billions of years, they glow for just **10,000** years.

The Crab Pulsar formed in a supernova that was recorded by stargazers around the world in **1054** CE.

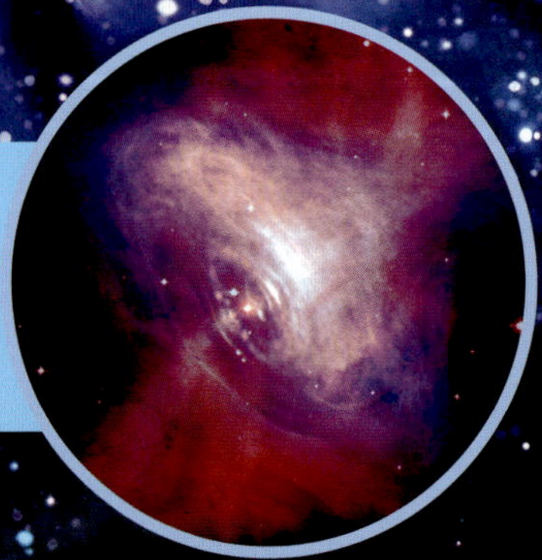

According to English physicist **Stephen Hawking**, black holes slowly lose energy and disappear over billions of years.

Stars that have large amounts of **heavy elements** from interstellar space shine more brightly, but have shorter lifespans.

Five of the brightest stars in the famous constellation of **Ursa Major** (the Great Bear) began life in the same open cluster.

The Milky Way galaxy has more than 150 globular clusters orbiting it, but the distant egg-shaped galaxy **M87** has more than 12,000!

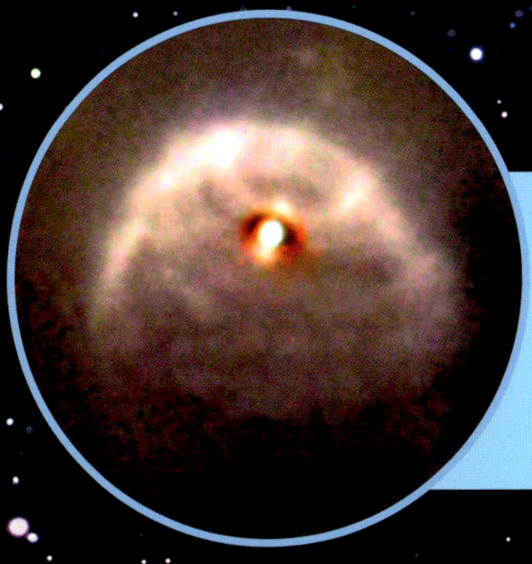

The closest star to Earth, a faint **red dwarf** called Proxima Centauri, is orbited by an Earth-like planet that could have water on its surface.

Your Questions Answered

Scientists now know an incredible amount about the stars, but space is still bursting with amazing information; there are always more questions to be answered. This is what makes people want to become scientists and astronauts, and to study space. Here are the answers to some interesting questions about space, then you can start asking more!

Who names the stars?

When people first started studying the sky they named the stars they could see and the patterns they made, after the shapes they thought they looked like or the position they held in the sky. The stars had different names in different languages and cultures.

Today, stars are given a name consisting of letters and numbers. This is so that they can be identified by anyone anywhere. An organization called the International Astronomical Union (IAU) controls naming of all objects or features that are discovered by astronomers.

How many stars are there?

There are so many, it is impossible to count! Our solar system is in a galaxy called the Milky Way, and scientists estimate that there are 100 billion stars in this galaxy alone. Then there are millions upon millions of galaxies in the Universe!

Where does the dust in space come from?

The dust in space is constantly being recycled as stars and planets go through their life cycles. Dust helps stars to form, and then is either blown away from the star by wind currents that move through space, or expelled in one go by a star explosion. The dust drifts through space again until it is swept up to become another star.

What are gas and dust clouds made from?

Although space can look empty, it's not. The space we see is actually filled with clouds of dust and gas. The dust is made up of tiny particles of elements such as carbon, iron, magnesium, and silicon. The gas is made up mainly of hydrogen and helium. Scientists spend a long time studying the dust in space, as it contributes to the creation of new planets and stars.

What is an atom?

Everything is made from atoms – they are the smallest parts that anything can be broken down into. Even a grain of sand is made up of millions of atoms all joined together. Atoms are too small to see with the naked eye, or even with a microscope. A single atom is made up of a nucleus, which contains protons and neutrons, and orbited by electrons.

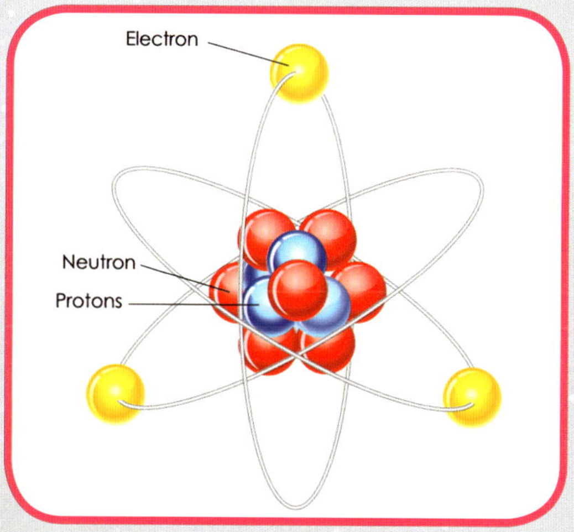

How do I become a space scientist?

The study of space is called astronomy, and space scientists are called astronomers. The most important subjects for an astronomer are the sciences, particularly physics, math, and chemistry. After school, you can go on to study astronomy or physics, or astrophysics—which is a combination of the two!

Glossary

asteroid A small rocky object made up of material left over from the birth of the solar system.

binary star One of a pair of stars orbiting each other.

black hole A superdense point in space, usually formed by a collapsed core of a giant star. A black hole's gravity is so powerful that even light cannot escape from it.

comet A chunk of rock and ice from the edge of the solar system. Close to the Sun, its melting ices form a coma and a tail.

exoplanet A planet orbiting a star outside our solar system.

galaxy A large system of stars, gas, and dust with anything from millions to trillions of stars.

globular cluster A dense ball of ancient, long-lived stars, found in orbit around galaxies, such as the Milky Way.

gravity A natural force created around objects with mass, which draws other objects toward them.

light-year The distance covered by light in a year—about 5.9 trillion miles (9.5 trillion km).

main sequence The longest phase in a star's life, when it shines by turning its main fuel source of hydrogen into helium at its core. During this time, the star's brightness and temperature are related—the brighter the star is, the hotter its surface and the bluer it looks.

Milky Way Our home galaxy, a spiral with a bar across its core. Our solar system is about 28,000 light-years from the monster black hole at its heart.

Moon Earth's closest companion in space, a ball of rock that orbits Earth every 27.3 days. Most other planets in the solar system have moons of their own.

multiple stars A system of two or more stars in orbit around one another.

nebula A cloud of gas or dust floating in space. Nebulae are the raw material used to make stars.

neutron star The core of a supermassive star, left behind by a supernova explosion and collapsed to the size of a city. Many neutron stars are also pulsars.

open cluster A large group of bright young stars that were born in the same nebula.

planet A world that orbits the Sun, which has enough mass and gravity to pull itself into a ball-like shape, and clear space around it of other large objects.

planetary nebula A growing cloud of glowing gas thrown off from the outer layers of a dying red giant star.

pulsar A fast-spinning neutron star whose intense magnetic field forces its radiation into two narrow beams that sweep around the sky like a lighthouse. From Earth, a pulsar appears as a quickly flashing star.

quasar A distant active galaxy with a very bright core.

red dwarf A small, faint star with a cool red surface and less than half the mass of the Sun.

red giant A huge, brilliant (very bright) star near the end of its life, with a cool, red surface. Red giants are stars that have used up the fuel supply in their core and are going through big changes in order to keep shining for a little longer.

satellite Any object orbiting a planet. Moons are natural satellites made of rock and ice. Artificial (manmade) satellites are machines in orbit around Earth.

supernova An enormous explosion marking the death of a star much more massive than the Sun.

supernova remnant An expanding (growing) cloud of shredded, superhot gas left behind a supernova explosion.

telescope A device that collects light or other radiations from space and uses them to create a bright, clear image. Telescopes can use either a lens or a mirror to collect light.

white dwarf The dense, burnt-out core of a star like the Sun, collapsed to the size of the Earth but still intensely hot.

Further Information

BOOKS

Daynes, Katie. *See Inside Space.* London, UK: Usborne Publishing, 2008.

De Amicis, Giulia. *In Orbit: Discovering the Solar System.* White Star, 2017.

DK Reference. *Space!* New York, NY: DK Publishing, 2015.

Murphy, Glenn. *Space: The Whole Whizz-Bang Story* (Science Sorted). New York, NY: Macmillan Children's Books, 2013.

Newman, Ben. *Professor Astro Cat's Frontiers of Space.* London, UK: Flying Eye Books, 2013.

Rogers, Simon. *Information Graphics: Space.* Somerville, MA: Big Picture Press, 2015.

WEBSITES

www.nasa.gov/kidsclub/index.html
Join Nebula at NASA Kids' Club to play games and learn about space.

www.ngkids.co.uk/science-and-nature/ten-facts-about-space
Get started with these ten great facts about space, then explore the rest of the National Geographic Kids site for more fun.

www.esa.int/esaKIDSen/
Explore this site from the European Space Agency. There's information, games, and news.

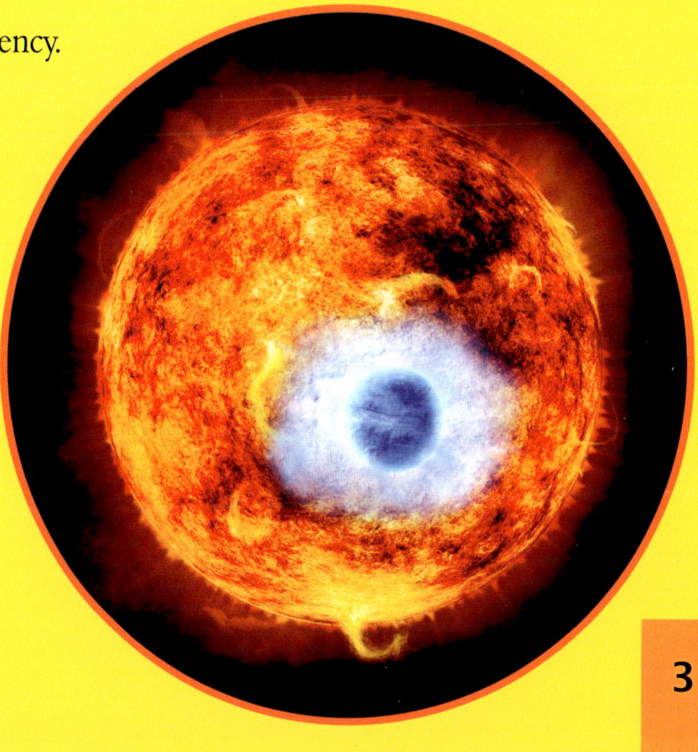

Index